JOEY and JET

TO ABBY AND SIMONE,
WHO LOVE A GOOD BOY-AND-DOG STORY

Atheneum Books for Young Readers • An imprint of Simon & Schuster Children's Publishing Division • 1230 Avenue of the Americas, New York, New York 10020 • Copyright © 2004 by James Yang • All rights reserved, including the right of reproduction in whole or in part in any form. • Book design by Polly Kanevsky • The text of this book is set in Tarzana. • The illustrations are rendered in digital pen and ink. • Manufactured in China • First Edition • 1 2 3 4 5 6 7 8 9 10 • Library of Congress Cataloging-in-Publication Data • Yang, James, 1960– • Joey and Jet / James Yang.—1st ed. • p.   cm. • "A Richard Jackson Book." • Summary: A boy and his dog play a game of fetch in a field of prepositions—among, between, past, and all around. • ISBN 0-689-86926-6 • [1. Play—Fiction. 2. Dogs—Fiction. 3. English language—Prepositions.] I. Title. • PZ7.Y1934Jo 2004 • [E]—dc22 • 2003016758

JOEY
and JET

James Yang

A Richard Jackson Book
Atheneum Books for Young Readers
new york london toronto sydney

This is Joey.

This is the ball.

This is Jet.

"Fetch!"

Jet chases the ball

among the birds . . .

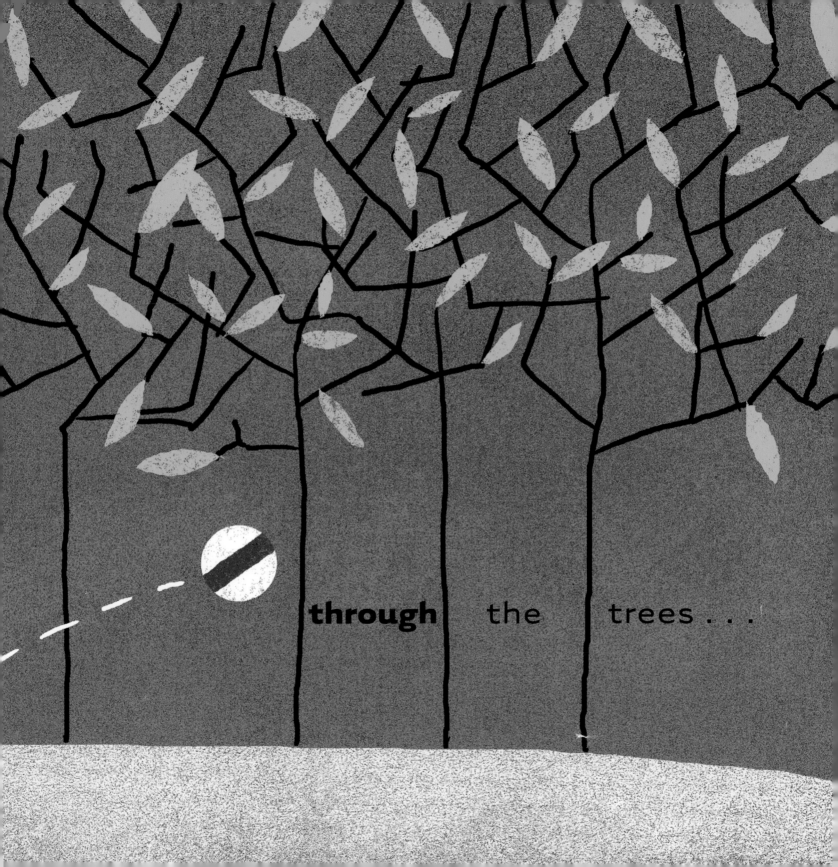

through the trees...

on

the water . . .

down
the
hill . . .

up

the

hill . . .

across the street . . .

between
the
tables...

over the roofs . . .

into
a
hole and . . .

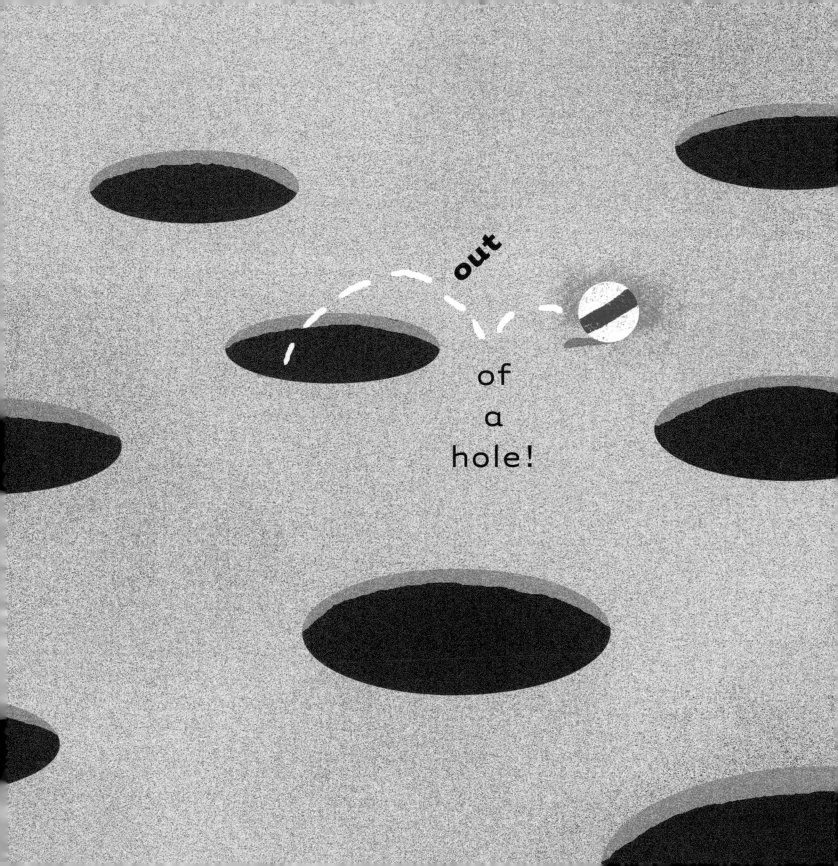

Jet found his ball and ran . . .

into
a
hole

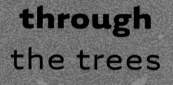

among
the
birds

through
the trees

on
the water

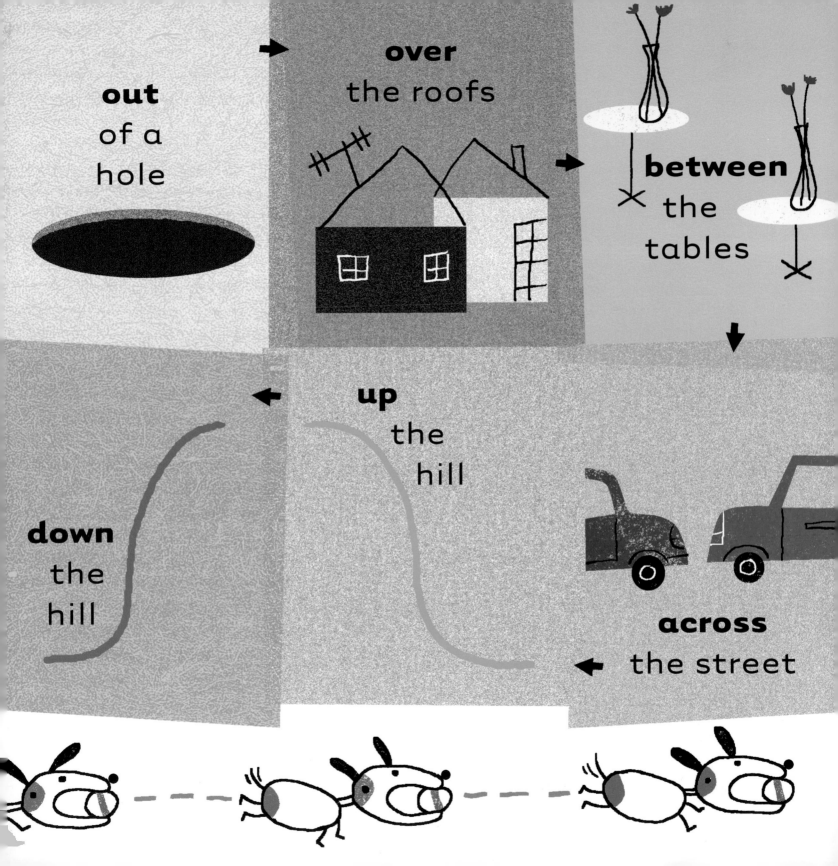

and back to Joey!

"Good boy!" said Joey.

Jet is the best ball chaser in the world.

A dog's work is never done.